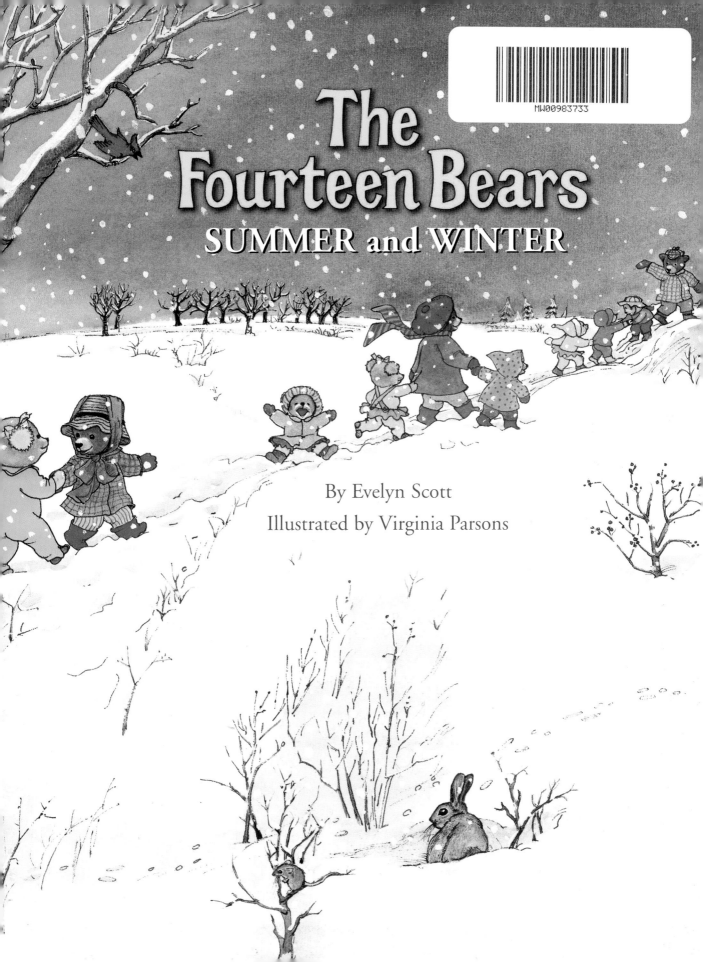

The Fourteen Bears

SUMMER and WINTER

By Evelyn Scott

Illustrated by Virginia Parsons

For Ursula
A REAL BEAR

Daddy Bear

Mother Bear

Little Theodore

Veronica   Virginia   Johanna   Ramona

Copyright © 1969, 1973 by Random House, Inc. All rights reserved under International and Pan-American Copyright Conventions. Published in the United States by Golden Books, an imprint of Random House Children's Books, a division of Random House, Inc., New York, and simultaneously in Canada by Random House of Canada Limited, Toronto. Originally published in 1969 and in 1973 in slightly different form by Western Publishing Company, Inc. Golden Books, A Golden Book, the G colophon, and the distinctive gold spine are registered trademarks of Random House, Inc.
Library of Congress Cataloging-in-Publication Data:
Scott, Evelyn.
The fourteen bears in summer and winter / by Evelyn Scott ; illustrated by Virginia Parsons.—1st Golden classic ed.   p. cm.
Originally published in 1969 and in 1973 in slightly different form by Western Pub. Co. under title: The fourteen bears, summer and winter.
"A Golden book."
Summary: A bear family amuses itself with summer and winter activities such as walking, swimming, making snowmen, and decorating trees.
ISBN: 0-375-83279-3 (trade)—ISBN: 0-375-93279-8 (lib. bdg.)
[1. Summer—Fiction. 2. Winter—Fiction. 3. Bears—Fiction.] I. Parsons, Virginia, ill. II. Title.
PZ7.S422Fo 2005   [E]—dc22   2004010816
www.goldenbooks.com
PRINTED IN MALAYSIA   First Golden Classic Edition 2005
10 9 8 7 6 5 4 3

Visit us on the Web! www.randomhouse.com/kids
Educators and librarians, for a variety of teaching tools, visit us at www.randomhouse.com/teachers

THE FOURTEEN BEARS in SUMMER

Hannah   Anna   Gloria   Emma   Henrietta   Flora   Dora

A GOLDEN BOOK • NEW YORK

Once upon a time, in a summer forest, there were fourteen bears.

There were the Daddy Bear and Little Theodore . . .

. . . and Victoria—that was the Mother Bear, and . . .

Virginia

Veronica

Ramona

Henrietta

Flora and Dora

Gloria

Emma

Anna

Johanna and Hannah.

They all lived in hollow trees.

All the trees
looked different
inside. One had
plump chairs
with fringe.

One had a velvet couch.

One had furniture
with painted flowers.

This one had
a modern couch.

This one had
a braided rug.

And this one had
a Chinese screen.

This bear's house
had a kitchen fireplace.

This bear's house
had a marble mantel.

And this bear's
house had a red
tile floor.

This bear's house was like a castle.

And this one was small and cozy.

Each bear had a separate tree house, except Little Theodore, because he was so little. He stayed with his mommy and daddy.

Every day the fourteen bears walked
paw in paw through the forest.
   And the birds sang, and the breeze
blew, and the sun beat on their ears.

When they got hot they went swimming in a big, deep, clear pool. There were lots of fish in the pool, but the bears never tried to catch them, so they were all good friends and played together.

Then the bears lay down on the warm
sand until their fur was dry and glistening.

When the bears were hungry, there was always lots of
honey. Flora had a honey farm with very special bees.

They made different flavors of honey: chocolate, vanilla, strawberry, maple, and sometimes coconut.

Then the fourteen bears walked home paw
in paw through the forest.

And the birds sang, and the breeze blew,
and the sun beat on their ears.

They climbed the branch steps,

and closed the bark doors.

VIRGINIA
PARSONS
ARTIST

When night came,
they went to bed.

And they slept

and slept

and slept

and slept

till morning.

All the bears,

from Anna

to Gloria,

had pleasant
dreams,

all the summer
night long.

And that's the
first story of the
fourteen bears.

Daddy Bear   Mother Bear   Veronica   Virginia   Johanna   Ramona

THE FOURTEEN BEARS in WINTER

Emma   Anna   Gloria   Hannah   Henrietta   Flora   Dora   Little Theodore

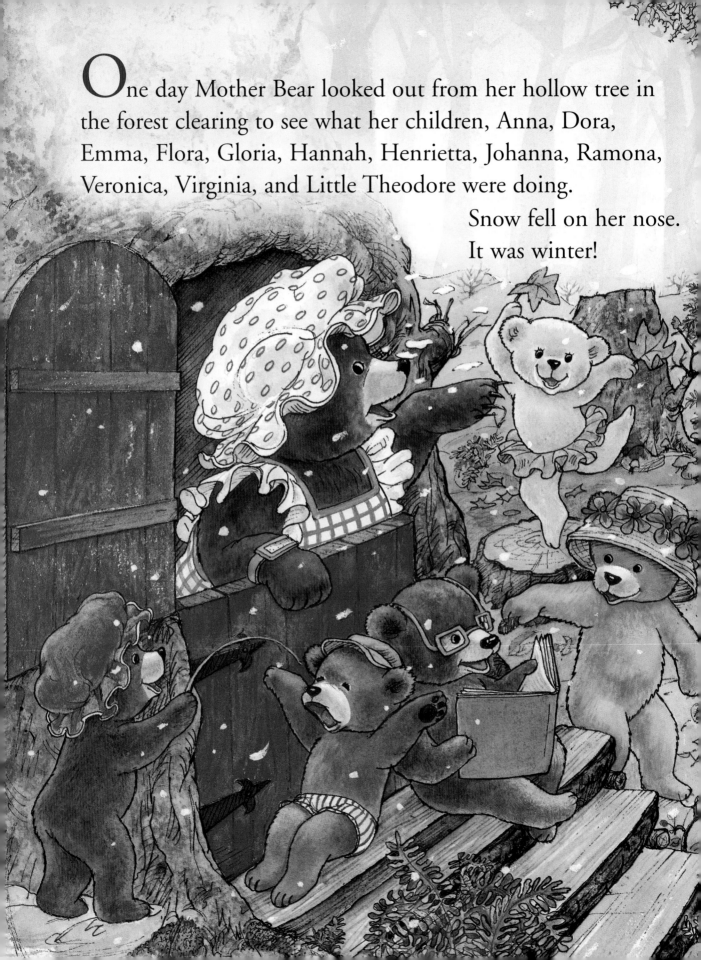

One day Mother Bear looked out from her hollow tree in the forest clearing to see what her children, Anna, Dora, Emma, Flora, Gloria, Hannah, Henrietta, Johanna, Ramona, Veronica, Virginia, and Little Theodore were doing.

Snow fell on her nose.
It was winter!

Father Bear hurried his family to bed
in their hollow trees.

After a fine two-month-long nap, Little Theodore began wriggling in the bed next to his parents' in the biggest hollow tree.

Mother Bear told him to go back to sleep. They were hi-ber-nat-ing. Little Theodore didn't know what hibernating meant. He didn't really know what winter meant.

So Father Bear said they could all put on

warm clothes, and go outside to find out.

Outside, everything was very white and bright and cold.

They all ran to their pond. It was frozen hard. The friendly fish were fast asleep, deep down in the mud.

Flora ran to her honey farm. The friendly
bees were snugly dreaming in their hives.

The fourteen bears began to walk paw in
paw through the forest. The winter sun beat on
their ears. Snow squeaked beneath their feet.

All at once the forest stopped. The bears stood staring at a farmyard and a big house. Right in front, there was a snowman wearing a large sign.

Henrietta, who had on her glasses, read the sign aloud:

WELCOME, NEIGHBORS. GONE TO GRANDMA'S.
MAKE YOURSELVES AT HOME.

"I don't believe that means us," said Mother Bear.

"Well, we're neighbors!" cried Little Theodore.

All the bear children were excited, there were such fine
playthings in the yard.

"We won't do any harm," said Father Bear.

So Flora pushed Dora in the swing.

Johanna, who loved to dance, put on skates
and skimmed across some ice.
Ramona found some bright red winter berries.

Father Bear and Little Theodore went skiing. Mother Bear
tried snowshoeing.

Emma, Hannah, and Veronica rode a sled down a hill and knocked the snowman flat!

Father Bear said the time had come to leave. They put all the playthings away. Then they built a bigger snowman. He looked just like Father Bear!

Last of all, they peeped into the house. Inside they saw a tree! It was hung with sparkling balls, golden stars, and silver rope.

Paw in paw, the fourteen bears walked back through the forest. Snow shook down on their ears. Sunset shimmered on their fur. In their clearing, they had just enough time before dark to hang ornaments on their trees.

Anna used the ruffle of a petticoat.

Virginia painted silver twigs
as far as she could reach.

Veronica tied hairbows to hers.

Johanna made some snowballs.
So did Father Bear.

Ramona set her holly on a branch.

Emma and Gloria hung out knitting wool.

Little Theodore gathered pine cones for Hannah, while she played her guitar.

Mother Bear scattered nuts and berries out for Flora and Dora, because they were half-asleep. Henrietta wrote down their adventure.

When it was quite dark, the bears climbed their branch steps and opened their bark doors and went back to bed.

All their trees had been trimmed
except the biggest one.

In the morning it was the most beautiful of all, hung with icicles.

Birds had eaten the nuts and berries from the snowy ground, and had hopped out a message.

SLEEP TIGHT
GOOD NIGHT
SEE YOU IN
THE SPRING

And that's the second story of the
fourteen bears.